**FRIENDS
OF ACPL**

jE
Car
Wis

**DO NOT REMOVE
CARDS FROM POCKET**

NANCY WHITE CARLSTROM

Wishing at Dawn in Summer

Illustrated by

DIANE WORFOLK ALLISON

Little, Brown and Company
Boston Toronto London

For David, only and always

N.W.C.

For Mickey

D.W.A.

Text copyright © 1993 by Nancy White Carlstrom
Illustrations copyright © 1993 by Diane Worfolk Allison

First Edition

Library of Congress Cataloging-in-Publication Data

Carlstrom, Nancy White.
    Wishing at dawn in summer / by Nancy White Carlstrom ; illustrated
by Diane Worfolk Allison. — 1st ed.
        p.   cm.
    Summary: A brother and sister have different wishes during an early
morning fishing trip.
    ISBN 0-316-12854-6
    [1. Brothers and sisters — Fiction. 2. Fishing — Fiction.
3. Wishes — Fiction.] I. Allison, Diane Worfolk, ill. II.Title.
    PZ.C21684WI 1993
    [E] — dc20   90-24877

10 9 8 7 6 5 4 3 2 1

SC
Published simultaneously in Canada by Little, Brown & Company
(Canada) Limited
Printed in Hong Kong

Kristina and I go fishing at dawn in summer.

We jump out of our beds onto the stone-cold floor,
waking up feetfirst.
Dressing in the pale purple light,
it doesn't matter if our socks match
or if we wash behind our ears.

"Ssh! Come on, Ken,
and don't wake the others,"
Kristina whispers.

We race down the path to the lake.
Our feet fly silently over well-packed sand and pine needles.
I think about how good the morning smells.
So fresh and wet.

Kristina beats me to the pier.
I say that's because she sleeps closest to the door
and I wear tie shoes.
We kneel, side by side,
on the worn wooden planks.
While we put our poles together,
I listen to the laughing of the lake
coming up through the cracks.

Kristina helps me attach the rooster tail lure
as we set our lines.
She says they're the best kind.
I don't know.
I just like the name. Rooster tail lure.

I wet my line, and Kristina reminds me
not to wiggle around so much.
"Relax," she says.
I dangle my feet over the edge
and make faces in the blue-black water.
Kristina thinks I'm afraid I won't catch a fish.
But I'm afraid I might.

Suddenly the sun comes up behind the mountain
and turns the whole lake pink.
I look out to the middle,
where a big fish jumps.
"Fish Wish!" I call.

It's a game Kristina and I play.
First one to see a fish jump
gets a wish.
I make my wish. Not out loud.

It's always the same.
I hope Kristina doesn't guess.
"I have a bite!" she says
and jerks the pole.
Then she starts to reel it in.

"Don't let the line go slack!" I tell her.
"I know, Ken," she says in her most impatient voice.
"I was the one who taught you how to fish. Remember?"
She's right, but it doesn't mean she'll catch this one.

"Oh, well. First bite gets first choice."
Kristina opens up the brown crumpled bag
and pulls out a smashed sandwich.
Made the night before and accidentally sat on.
But even peanut butter sandwiches,
flattened and stiff,
taste good
when we're watching the fish jump
and the sky roll over.

We move our lines through the water.
To trick the rainbow trout,
Kristina says.
Two clouds ride piggyback on the mountain.
The sun bursts out above the clouds,
and now the lake is glass.
Our faces stare back, golden.

We sing a dawning song.
Kristina says it's for the sun and the mountain
and the sky.
I sing for the rainbow trout.
But I don't tell Kristina.

I'm sure I see him eyeing me
from the smooth surface.
He hears my song
and flashes, free and shining.
Alive!

When we know that the day will be hot,
and our bottoms are getting tired of sitting,
we pull our lines out of the water.
Drips fall, *plip-plop,* onto the planks.
Kristina yanks off her rooster tail lure
and puts it away.
"Let's go, Ken. We'll catch that rainbow trout another day."

I say, "Okay."
But think,
Not if I have wishes.